For Nana Sue
Shine On!

Sheree Fitch 2005

If I Were the Moon

Text by Sheree Fitch
Illustrations by Leslie Elizabeth Watts

Doubleday Canada Limited

For Gilles, today et au-delà
— S.F.

For Laura and Emma Wilkes,
and Madison LeQuelenec of Alliston,
and Nicholas and Jaclyn Lucyk of Napanee,
with love from Aunt Leslie
— L.W.

Copyright © 1999 Sheree Fitch (text)
Copyright © 1999 Leslie Elizabeth Watts (illustrations)

Canadian Cataloguing in Publication Data

Fitch, Sheree
  If I were the moon

Poems.
ISBN 0-385-25744-9

I. Watts, Leslie Elizabeth, 1961-   . II. Title.

PS8561.I86I3 1999   jc811'.54   C98-932819-8
PR9199.3.F5713 1999

Designed by Andrew Smith Graphics Inc.
Printed and bound in Canada

Published in Canada by
Doubleday Canada Limited
105 Bond Street
Toronto, Ontario
M5B 1Y3

FRI 10 9 8 7 6 5 4 3 2 1

If I were the moon,
I'd shine down my light

Right into your bedroom
To warm up the night.

If I were the ocean,
I'd sail you away

Then bring you back home
At the end of the day.

If I were a tree,
I'd let you climb high

You could talk to the squirrels
And tickle the sky.

If I were a flower,
I'd grow just for you

I'd dance in the wind
When you wanted me to.

If I were a snowflake,
I'd tickle your face
Then blow away laughing
In white open space.

If I were a rainbow,
I'd let you ride down

My kaleidoscope slide
All the way to the ground.

If I were a mountain,
You could reach for the sky
Then sing to the angels
While clouds drifted by.

If I were a song,
I'd hum you to sleep.

I'd give you a dream
All your own just to keep.

But I am who I am,
And that's even better.

We'll all be together
Today
　　　and for ever . . .

. . . and after